SWASHBUCKLING
ADVENTURE

MEET NELLY, THE IRREPRESSIBLE
HEROINE, AND HER BEST FRIEND,
A TURTLE CALLED COLUMBUS.

AHOY AERONAUTS!

DARING DEEDS AWAIT!

JOIN THE RIDE, FROM THE
HIGHEST HEIGHTS TO THE
DEEPEST DEPTHS.

FOR BENJAMIN

OXFORD
UNIVERSITY PRESS

Great Clarendon Street, Oxford OX2 6DP
Oxford University Press is a department of the University of Oxford.
It furthers the University's objective of excellence in research, scholarship,
and education by publishing worldwide. Oxford is a registered trade mark
of Oxford University Press in the UK and in certain other countries

British Library Cataloguing in Publication Data

Data available

ISBN: 978-0-19-274271-1

1 3 5 7 9 10 8 6 4 2

Printed in Great Britain by Bell and Bain Ltd, Glasgow

Paper used in the production of this book is a natural,
recyclable product made from wood grown in sustainable forests.
The manufacturing process conforms to the environmental
regulations of the country of origin.

Nelly

and the Flight of
the Sky Lantern

BY ROLAND CHAMBERS

ILLUSTRATED BY ELLA OKSTAD

OXFORD
UNIVERSITY PRESS

CHAPTER ONE

Hanging from the wall in Nelly's bedroom was a map of the world and everything in it, with the North Pole at the top and the South Pole at the bottom. All the most important bits were in the right places (so far as Nelly knew), except that whereas the world is round, this map was flat and made of wool: a brilliantly-coloured blanket that Nelly's mother had woven her when she was a baby.

It was Nelly's first map; the one that had shown her what camels look like and where you can find them, as well as tigers, giant anteaters, and the terrible Komodo dragon. If she stood up

close, she could count the horsey zebras that ran all over Africa, and a single yeti in the Himalayas, standing on top of the tallest mountain with an expression on its face as if it were wondering what it was doing there.

At the centre of the tapestry was Nelly's home, woven so finely that she could make out the red tiles on the roof and the curtains on the windows, and in the sitting room, her mother, Mrs. Peabody, knitting, just as she always knitted. If Nelly crossed her eyes, she could see each woollen stitch, like a hairy grain of rice: thousands of them, hundreds of thousands. And then she stepped back and the grains dissolved

into deserts and jungles, lakes and rivers, continents and oceans: the whole world stretched before her as if she were high in the sky looking down—a bird, a cloud.

As a little girl, Nelly would look at the map for hours, with her faithful turtle, Columbus, sitting beside her. She would admire the tall ships sailing around the Horn of Africa, and wonder where her father was—Captain Bones Peabody, who had sailed away the day after Nelly was born on a voyage of zoological and botanical discovery, and had not returned.

She would wonder where his ship was anchored, or if it was already at the bottom of the sea, until one day she went to look for him in a boat with knitted sails, and only Columbus to keep her company.

Nelly found her father living inside a volcano at the North Pole, and had so many adventures along the way, she could have filled a book with them. She met his colleagues, the so-called Gentlemen of the Exploratory Flotilla, and his crew who worshipped him as a god. But she didn't stay long, because she had promised her mother she would be home in a year, so back she went, taking her father's promise that he would follow as soon as he was able.

Nelly sailed home, through storms and around whirlpools, and along the way she thought of the tapestry on her bedroom wall, and in the middle of it, the little house

with its red roof and green windows. She pictured the things she had left behind: the beach with rock pools full of crabs and starfish, the rhubarb patch and the apple tree her mother had planted for her when she was a baby. She missed the sound of her mother knitting, clickety-click, clickety-clack, and most of all the person doing the knitting: Mrs Peabody sitting in her favourite armchair at the centre of the world.

But when Nelly finally dropped anchor at the end of her adventure, her mother wasn't there to meet her. Only the retired cabin boy Nelly had hired to look after her while she was away. The one from the Fiennes,

6

Hilary, and Scott catalogue, which supplies explorers with everything necessary for the launching of an expedition.

CLICKETY-CLICK
CLICKETY-CLACK

'Ahoy shipmate!' he called, when Nelly ran into the sitting room.

'Ahoy nothing!' said Nelly. 'Where's Mrs Peabody?'

'Hoity-toity!' said the cabin boy, and reaching into his dressing gown (which was actually Captain Peabody's dressing gown) he produced a note in Nelly's mother's handwriting.

Gone to visit granny, back soon.

Except that Nelly didn't have a granny. Not a granny, at least, that she had ever heard of.

CHAPTER TWO

Nelly never called a disaster a disaster before it was absolutely necessary. If it was raining, she put on a raincoat. If she lost a button, she let it go, because a button is just a button. Faced with something more serious, she made a plan and stuck to it, however difficult or dangerous the undertaking, because that was the sort of person Nelly was. It was part of her code.

But on this occasion she did not have a plan, or any idea of how to make one, because her mother had left no forwarding address, or any proper explanation for her disappearance, and when Nelly asked the retired cabin boy how long she had been away already, he just shrugged. He said he was an old sailor, who had answered an

advert in a respectable catalogue; an advert which he produced from the other pocket of Captain Peabody's dressing gown.

CABIN BOY WANTED, it read, START IMMEDIATELY.

Except that when he had arrived at Nelly's address, there was nobody there.

'You mean you've been living on your own all this time?' gasped Nelly.

And the cabin boy nodded, so that his grey hair fell over his ears. He said he had lived like a hermit crab for a year, and that he was so relieved to see another human face it made him want to cry. In fact he looked so unhappy, Nelly felt almost sorry for him, until she noticed that he was wearing her mother's slippers.

'Don't you have any clothes of your own?' she snapped, and hugging Columbus close to her chest, she went upstairs to her bedroom to think things through.

That evening Nelly sat looking at the tapestry on her wall; the one she had had ever since she was a tiny baby. There were the walruses off the coast of Greenland and the tall ships rounding the Horn of Africa. There were the spouting whales and the delightful penguins, and at the centre of it all the tiny figure of her mother, sitting in her usual seat, except that the real Mrs Peabody wasn't there. Nelly's mother, who had never wandered further than the vegetable garden, to sing a little song to the well by the apple tree, perhaps, or to check on the rhubarb. Who could sometimes be found standing in a rock pool in her night dress or at the top of the lighthouse, gazing out to sea, but mostly liked to stay indoors, with the curtains half drawn, knitting or doing the crossword puzzle.

'Where have you got to?' Nelly whispered to the woman in the tapestry, but of course woollen mothers do not speak; and in fact Nelly's real mother had never talked much either. She had never mentioned a granny, or any other relatives either, and Nelly had never bothered to ask. And now her mother was gone, vanished like a magician's penny, making Nelly wonder what it would be like to be an orphan like her father.

'Although what's the point of having parents,' she asked Columbus, 'if they're always wandering off and keeping secrets?'

But Columbus didn't answer, because he had fallen asleep on Nelly's pillow. So Nelly sat on her bed, looking at the tapestry, listening to the sound of knitting needles drifting up through the cracks in her floorboards (although it wasn't her mother knitting) until she was sleeping too.

ZZZZZZZZZZZ

CHAPTER THREE

That night there was a storm so violent it blew the apples off the apple tree, but Nelly didn't notice, because she was asleep with Columbus beside her on the pillow, and Columbus was no ordinary turtle. When he was awake, it is true, he wasn't particularly courageous; not much good with a cutlass or a pistol in the heat of battle. But when he was asleep he dreamed amazing dreams, and sometimes Nelly dreamed them too. About things that were hidden in the past or the future: the shape of the adventure to come.

Now Nelly dreamed of a room made of iron, with a low ceiling and no windows. With a four-poster bed against one wall, and a wardrobe against another, and against a third, a girl, sitting at a desk. Whatever

she was writing about must have been very interesting, because she didn't pause, or look up. She just sat with her feet tucked under the chair, scribbling away.

And then she shut the book and Nelly, peering over her shoulder, saw what was written on the front cover.

THIS DIARY BELONGS TO PENELOPE PORBEAGLE

At the top was a picture of a hot-air balloon, and at the bottom, a submarine, both cut out of paper and coloured in crayons. They made a very pleasing design, and for a moment the girl in the dream sat back and admired her own handiwork, before locking the diary away in a drawer and hiding the key inside one of the posts of her bed. Then she hopped under the covers, and when she turned out the light, Nelly woke up in her own room, feeling her mother so close it made her hair stand on end.

Nelly expected to find Mrs Peabody standing right next to her pillow—but she wasn't. She wasn't under the bed, either, or behind the curtains, or in the wardrobe, or out on the landing where the moon cast long, black shadows. Down in the hall the grandfather clock said twelve and the family portraits hanging from the walls

seemed to follow Nelly with their eyes. But when she stopped in front of the portrait of Mrs Peabody, it didn't come to life, as she half expected. It stared out of the frame with no expression at all, as if to say, 'Look somewhere else.'

So Nelly looked. In the door to the sitting room, where the cabin boy was asleep in the chair by the window. In the dining room and the cloakroom. She opened all the drawers in the kitchen in case her mother was nestled between the spoons, and checked in the bathroom where Mrs Peabody's shower cap hung in the dark like a jellyfish. But she didn't find what she was looking for until she walked up the steep stairs to the attic and opened the trap door.

Above Nelly's head, the storm had torn a jagged hole in the roof, and through it the moon shone white and fierce. It shone on the bits and pieces of old furniture—a cot, a low table, a little chair. On the nails that pinned the floorboards and on the wicker basket in which Mrs Peabody kept her wool—a mountain of it piled up in every colour.

Now the sky had cleared, so that when Nelly climbed into the basket and lay on her back, she could look up and see the stars. Outside the ocean rustled like leaves and beneath her the house made little creaks and groans. Occasionally a light breeze would ruffle her hair, but she wasn't cold. She was as warm and comfortable as an unborn baby, and she might have fallen fast asleep then and there, listening to the sound of the waves and her own heart beating. She might have slept and dreamed something else that made her forget the dream she'd had before, and then perhaps everything would have been different, but she didn't because as she snuggled deeper

into the wool, she discovered that most of it had already been knitted.

Nelly couldn't tell what sort of knitting it was until she had climbed out of the basket and pulled it all onto the floor. It wasn't a blanket or a tapestry, or a tent or a sail. It had no corners she could see, but when she had unpacked the whole thing, she saw that it was connected to the basket by ropes like a kite. But it wasn't a kite, either. More like a gigantic sack, or an enormous egg cosy.

And then Nelly knew what it was, because Columbus had shown it to her in her dream. A balloon. A hot-air balloon, knitted in multicoloured stripes as though it had been coloured in crayon. And stowed in the bottom of the basket, a map, a book (**A Guide to Hot Air and Airships**), and a knitted flying suit that fitted Nelly perfectly.

CHAPTER  FOUR

Nelly didn't like to wait about once her mind was made up. In the attic of her house was a balloon, and inside it, a map. Above it the storm had torn a convenient hole: an unmistakable invitation to an adventure. All that remained was to gather the things she needed and be off, so Nelly gathered her things. She collected her turtle from her room, and also her red-handled cutlass. She crept down to the kitchen and raided the larder, then out to her ship and salvaged the ship's stove, along with her telescope, kettle, and compass. She did not go back to bed. She worked through the night, beneath the stars, and she didn't feel a little bit sleepy.

Nelly worked as quickly and as silently as

possible, so as not to wake the retired cabin boy. Once she dropped a cup, but managed to catch it before it smashed on the floor. There was a scuffle with the stove. When the grandfather clock in the hallway struck three, it made her jump, but he didn't wake. He sat sleeping in his chair by the sitting room window with his mouth open, snoring gently, while Nelly slipped a second note into his dressing gown pocket.

'Gone to find Mother,' it said. 'Back soon.'

Then she went upstairs and studied A Guide to Hot Air and Airships until the clock in the hall struck five and it was time to open the throat of her balloon and let the whispering wind slide in.

Have you ever stood in the attic of your own house and seen the stars through the roof, twinkling like distant bonfires, and known that in a few minutes you will be amongst them? It is an extraordinary feeling. It takes your breath away. It takes the whole world's breath away, and what it does with that breath is to put it into the ghost of a dream that is rising from the floor around you, first in low rolling hills and valleys, then in mountains, and as the mountains flow together, into a single rippling wave that grows upward into a teardrop-shaped phantom, with its sides stroked by starlight and its insides glowing with the fire from a little stove that once boiled a kettle in the kitchen of a ship captained by a girl called Nelly. Nelly Peabody, who now stood beside her new ship, ticking things off her list.

☐ One frying pan.

☐ One tapestry from bedroom wall.

☐ One red-handled cutlass
(courtesy of previous adventures).

☐ One turtle, Columbus, with his head firmly stuck in his shell.

Nelly watched the balloon grow until it stood tall above her, so that all she could see was the curved inside, lit up with orange, as it tugged at the anchor rope that held it to the floorboards.

'I name you *The Sky Lantern*,' she said, and making sure one last time that everything she needed was safely aboard, climbed into the basket, cut the ropes with her red-handled cutlass, and was off.

CHAPTER
FIVE

If you had been standing outside the house that morning, in the garden, or on the quay, what you would have seen was this: the last stars so faint, you would hardly have been able to make them out at all, like freckles of salt, and floating up into them, a majestic form, large, slow, and weightless, lifting slowly above the chimney tops—the sky already streaked with red.

Nelly saw the attic floor drawing away from her, along with the broken-down rocking chair, cot, and spindle. She saw the hole in the roof, which was her escape hatch, and for a moment a face looking up at her. A grey face with dark smudges for eyes—the cabin boy. But then he was gone, and the hole was just a hole, and soon not even that: just a pinprick in Nelly's red roof.

Nelly floated up from the house she was born in, and everything opened out beneath her. She saw her boat on the water, and the beach with rock pools in it. She saw the apple tree stripped of apples, and the rhubarb patch, and the dry well which her mother liked to sing to.

And then everything blurred together, and at the same time separated out into the land and the ocean—a sea of green next to another sea of blue—and Nelly was in the sky, which didn't feel like sky any more. Just open space, vast and empty, and rising up to join her the morning sun, like the mother of all hot-air balloons.

'Look!' she shouted, holding Columbus in her arms, so that he could take in the view. And Columbus looked, but didn't seem to like what he saw, perhaps because a turtle is not an up-in-the-air sort of creature. So she folded him into her tapestry, which was like a blanket, and put the kettle on.

There is nothing wrong with a breakfast of corned beef and black tea, wherever you take it, especially if the corned beef is eaten with fried potatoes and tomatoes. But when the same breakfast is eaten aboard a hot-air balloon soaring a mile above the ocean it is another matter entirely: when the kettle has been boiled and the potatoes fried on the same cooker that keeps you afloat. Then it is a miracle.

Nelly floated in silence. There was no hum of canvas or rigging as there would have been aboard a ship. The balloon was just a bag full of sky a little warmer than the rest of the sky. It drifted on the wind, out to sea, which was where Nelly wanted to go, and for a while she was happy just to stand and enjoy the feeling of moving in the right direction. She looked above her, and there was nothing but blue. She looked below her and the waves were so small they were just specks of sunlight, winking on and off. She listened to the seagulls, and watched the clouds, like small puffs from invisible cannons, turn white. Then she ate her breakfast and had a snooze, and when she woke the sun was halfway up the sky and she was hungry again. So she switched off the flame of her cooker, and when the balloon was close enough to the water, fetched out her fishing rod.

CHAPTER SIX

Nelly knew from Captain Peabody's book that hot-air balloons float because the air inside them is lighter than the air outside. But a balloon is like a bubble: you cannot steer it in the same way that you steer a ship. You cannot set a course against the wind, only run in front of it, so if you want to change direction you will have to find another wind.

And this was why Nelly's wind map was so special. It showed the land and the sea as other maps do, but over them Mrs Peabody had drawn hundreds of arrows, chasing one another in swirls like an unwinding fingerprint. Here and there were numbers, which showed the height at which each wind blew, and that afternoon

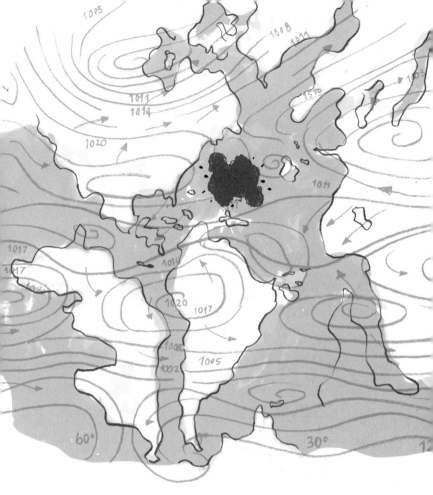

Nelly practised using it. If she turned up the flame of her cooker, she went higher. If she turned it down she drifted lower. And at each height she discovered different winds, or rather, the same wind blowing in different directions.

'Just as if,' she explained to Columbus, 'the sky were a basket and the wind were really a jumble of wool, winding under and over itself.'

But of course Columbus didn't answer, because he was feeling unwell. So Nelly let him be, while she mastered the art of drifting in the right direction, checking her height against her barometer: an instrument which on land can be used to predict the weather, but in the air measures altitude— the distance between a girl and the rustling sea—just by weighing the sky.

Nelly practised all afternoon and after supper went to sleep in her flying suit, wrapped up in the blanket her mother had woven for her, drifting high on an easterly wind. When she woke in the middle of the night, she lay looking at *The Sky Lantern*'s inside, lit up by the homely fire

of her cooker, with the stars all around her
and the moon leading her on. And when she
went back to sleep it was like falling asleep
in her mother's arms, except of course her
mother wasn't there. Only Columbus and
the things her mother had made for her,
including the wind map, which showed
Nelly's destination as a splodge of red.

It was not usual, Nelly knew, to mark

a destination with a blob of red ink. It is more common to use an 'X', as in 'X marks the spot'. But she didn't let it bother her. Far behind her was her house with the cabin boy in it, who would look after things while she was away. In front of her was her adventure, whatever it might be. Everything was in its right place.

Nelly lived like that day after day, following the wind, hunting up and down in the sky for the right breeze, practising her aeronautical manoeuvres until she was such an excellent balloonist that she could do a figure of eight as easily as tying her shoe laces. At night she slept as wild geese do, on the wing, and in the morning she took her balloon down to the level of the sea, so that the waves almost touched the basket, and lowered her ship's bucket so that she could wash and make tea (using a special tea bag that could suck the salt out of sea water). She lived quite happily like that for weeks and weeks, until one day, feeling a little cramped and hot, she wondered if it might be all right to take a swim.

It was such an attractive idea that she didn't doubt it. It was early morning. The sun was up, but the air was still. The surface of the sea was absolutely flat, like a bath, and Nelly thought how wonderful it would be to jump in, because why not? And get a little exercise. She would tie a rope round her middle and splash about in the ocean, and when she was finished, Columbus could have a bath too.

It was the sort of idea you have when you are not thinking very clearly, or not really thinking at all. When you are just dreaming about thinking, because a balloon is not a diving platform. It doesn't sit around while you splash about—or not necessarily. But Nelly stripped off anyway, and at first everything went beautifully. In she dived and the water was delicious—cool and clear—and so wide and empty. It was wonderful to stretch her arms and legs, to dive beneath the surface, and come up blowing like a dolphin. When she lay on her back, she could see her balloon, floating a few feet above her head, and when she trod water, she could turn in a circle and see the ocean, all the way to the horizon. Except that when she looked closely, she realised there was something in it.

One minute Nelly was happily splashing about. The next she noticed something off to her right. At first it seemed a long way off: a shadow. Something just under the water. Something rushing towards her so fast she hardly had time to scramble up the rope and into the basket before her balloon jumped into the air like a startled cat.

CHAPTER SEVEN

Hot-air balloons do not usually spring into the air like startled cats, but Nelly's did. It jumped as if it had a life of its own to save, so that it was just luck that Nelly fell back into the basket and not out of it. But her relief at escaping a hungry shark or curling tentacle lasted only as long as it took her to realize that the danger was from above and not below. That the thing racing towards her over the water was the shadow of a storm come out of nowhere while she was busy dreaming: a cloud that was sucking at the ocean and the air above like an angry giant breathing in.

When Nelly had been captain of a ship, she had weathered storms by trimming her canvas and bailing with a bucket. But a hot-air balloon has no rudder. It has no sails (or only a hollow one, like a sack). It simply goes where the wind blows, and now the wind was blowing upwards and Nelly went with it.

In the time it takes to say 'batten down the hatches', she was inside the storm itself, but she didn't lose her head for a second, because that was not the sort of person Nelly was. Faced with a calamity, she did not scream more than was necessary, or curse things that were not alive. She did not panic just because she was dressed in nothing but her underpants as the rain turned to chunks of ice the size of tennis balls. Checking the needle of her barometer, she saw that she had climbed two thousand feet in under a minute and was still climbing, but she did not jump overboard, or become hysterical. She simply pulled on her woollen flying suit, buttoned up her sou'wester and clapped a saucepan on her head to protect it from the hail. Then she wrapped her arms around Columbus and told him not to worry, because a storm is not a crocodile or a dragon. It does not actually want to kill you or eat you, and although it sometimes seems as though it will go on forever, it will eventually come to an end just like anything else. It will blow itself out or reach its natural

limit, because there is no such thing as a storm as big as the world.

Nelly spoke to Columbus, not with words (which the storm could snatch away) but in her mind, where he was sure to hear her. She told him that a storm has walls and a ceiling, and all he needed to do was sit tight. That a hurricane is a lot of bother about nothing, and as soon as it was over, she would put the kettle on. She invited him to snuggle a little deeper into the eiderdown, so that he would be sure of keeping warm and safe, while all around the lightning fizzed and thunder cracked—BANG!—as if somebody were smashing a hole in the sky.

Nelly shot up so fast she had to hold her nose and blow to clear her ears. At five thousand feet, the ropes of the balloon began to freeze. At ten her nails turned blue. At fifteen thousand feet the air became so thin it was hard to breathe, but Nelly kept thinking comforting thoughts. She pictured

the storm and *The Sky Lantern* shooting up through the middle of it, with its brave flame flickering and its basket swinging below. She pictured the sky above the storm, clear and blue, and sang a sea shanty ('Hooray and up she rises') as loudly as she could to keep her spirits strong. She shouted at the storm as the barometer came close to what balloonists call 'the death zone', but just as the needle swung past twenty thousand feet, the balloon popped out through the roof of the clouds into a silence so complete it was shocking.

Nelly no longer knew what to say or how to think. Below her was the storm, with light flickering inside it. Above her was her balloon, and all around was the sky, so empty she did not dare to look at it. she floated at the top of the world, and if she had gone much higher, she might have fallen out of it altogether. But she didn't. She stayed where she was, adjusting to the thinness of the air, and to the blankness of the light—the whiteness of it—which gradually turned blue as her eyes got used to it. A deep, beautiful blue, and very far off, a little black speck getting bigger as Nelly watched.

'Perhaps it's a shark?' she thought dreamily, but of course it wasn't, because sharks do not swim at twenty thousand feet above sea level.

'Or a bird?' But it didn't have any wings. It was long, sleek, and grey, with little fins at the back: a ship that slipped through the sky as gracefully as a whale slips through water. An airship—a zeppelin—driven against the wind by a tiny propeller, and beneath it,

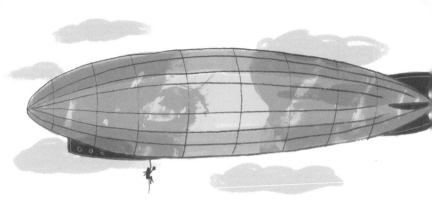

a wooden cabin with round glass portholes.

'Oh look!' said Nelly, as a trapdoor opened, 'somebody's coming.'

And down towards her came a man at the end of a rope, like a spider on its thread. But Nelly wasn't frightened, although she didn't like spiders. She just watched until he had lowered himself all the way down and was dangling in the air in front of her, his blue eyes blinking behind his goggles. And then he reached inside the jacket of his flying suit and pulled out a map. A delicate, hand-drawn map, with a cross in the middle and written underneath it, an explanation.

'You are here.'

CHAPTER EIGHT

Nelly's fellow balloonist sat at the end of his rope on a sling of canvas. He wore a leather helmet with flaps for his ears, thick leather gloves and his spindly legs (encased in warm leather trousers) were crossed at the knee, as if he were sitting in his favourite armchair. He had an expression on his face that suggested he was very interested indeed to make Nelly's acquaintance, but he didn't try to speak. He just looked at her through his goggles, leaning forward and blinking, as if waiting for her to begin.

'Thank you,' said Nelly, 'but I already know where I am. I'm just not quite sure if I know where I'm going.'

And she took out her wind map, with the destination marked in red.

'Except, perhaps it isn't a destination at all,' she explained, scratching it with her fingernail. 'Perhaps it's just an accident. You know, like a blob of jam.'

And now that Nelly came to think about it properly, it seemed very possible. A blob of jam or redcurrant jelly her mother had spilled over breakfast. Perhaps she had floated off on a wild goose chase (or a jam and jelly chase), and had only realized it just now, twenty thousand feet above sea level, a thousand miles from home, because she had met a stranger who had been kind enough to take an interest in her.

Nelly stood in her basket while the man examined her map. The air was so thin, it made her pant. She was cold and giddy, but most of all she was embarrassed. She looked at the top of his head and wished he would just tell her what she already knew. That she was a fool. That she had come a long way for nothing. But when he looked up, he was smiling. He just looked at her through his goggles, blinking his blue eyes slowly, and then—taking his hand from one of his fleece-lined gloves—he pointed down.

CHAPTER

NINE

Now the storm had slipped away, and what was left was nothing—miles of it— and down below, the Earth, wrapped in a swirl of its own breath. The World, not flat any more, but round, so that she could see the bend of the horizon, and the sea, not a simple sheet of blue, but different colours and textures, the deeps almost black, the shallows green as copper—wide open spaces dark and clear as jelly.

'Oh,' said Nelly, and taking out her telescope, she looked more closely: the water like a pane of glass, so that she could see what was underneath. Reefs of coral. A pod of whales. A glitter of silver, which might have been a shoal of sardines or a million silver coins. And there, directly beneath her, a red stain, as if the water itself were bleeding.

'Look!' shouted Nelly, glancing up at her companion, but the man was already spinning himself back up towards the cabin of his ship, leaving Nelly alone again, with her destination below her: a red spot so large she could see it with her naked eye, and in the middle of it (when she looked through her telescope again) somebody waving.

'Impossible,' she whispered, but she wasn't mistaken. Far, far below was a figure —a tiny silhouette—waving at her, as if to say, 'Hello up there! Come down!'

And Nelly waved back, jumping and yelling as the wind snatched her voice away.

'I'm coming, I'm coming!' she shouted,

but the breeze that took her words was blowing her along with it, too, and it made her desperate.

'Wait!' she screamed 'Wait!'

But it was she who was drifting, leaving the figure behind, filling her with such a homesick longing that she wanted to climb up onto the rim of the basket and jump.

'I'm here!' she shouted. 'I'm here!' but the figure only waved, and Nelly

couldn't bear it, because she felt certain she knew who it was.

'Come down! Come down!' it called—a tiny speck—and she could hear her mother's voice, and see her face.

So she jumped.

Nelly jumped from twenty thousand feet and fell like a diving bird or an arrow, taking the tiny pinprick of red below her as her target. She fell with the sound of the wind roaring in her ears, her stomach turning over and over, and her brain not really believing she had jumped at all. One part of it was saying, 'No, no, no, no!' as another whooped with joy because falling from so high up was like flying, and for a long time she could pretend that she really was. Flying like a stooping bird or a falling stone, although the fall

was so great it was possible to pretend she was not falling at all.

Nelly fell in a straight line. She did not weave the wind, as she would have done in a balloon, or plot a course. She plummeted to Earth like a blazing star, with a picture of her mother in her head, until the ocean began rushing up to meet her, closer and closer, so that she could see the frothy peaks of the waves. Then she let her woollen tapestry open above her—whoomp!—and she was floating in silence. The wind no longer roared. Her brain no longer screamed. Her heart beat fast in her chest, and as it slowed she had time to look down between her dangling feet at the world below. The ocean criss-crossed with the wakes of sailing ships. The sea of red in the sea of blue. A figure waving at her, but not her mother, as she had hoped. A boy, standing on a large green platform, surrounded by a rail. A boy on a buoy, getting larger as Nelly floated down towards him, waving his arms, but not in a friendly way. Waving frantically and shouting instructions as the waves, once again, began rushing up to meet her.

'Left!' shouted the boy. 'Left! Left! *Left!*'

'All right!' shouted Nelly, 'I'm doing my best!'

And then she was down, ten yards or so from the buoy itself.

'I said left!' shouted the boy.

'So you said left,' said Nelly, clambering up a metal ladder onto the deck, feeling that somehow, in the excitement of the moment, she had forgotten something very important. But just as she remembered what it was (and before she could properly panic), out of the sky, on the end of a rope, came a rusty bucket, and inside it, one duffel bag and one turtle.

60

CHAPTER

TEN

Nelly didn't want to talk at first. She wanted to sit with Columbus on her lap and catch her breath. But the boy talked enough for two. He wanted to know who Nelly was and where she came from, and what she was doing jumping out of a balloon at twenty thousand feet with nothing but a knitted eiderdown for a parachute. He wanted to explain why she was so foolish for not listening to his advice, because he was a great expert on parachutes and on several other things besides. He knew all about windspeed, for example, and why silk was a great deal more useful than wool, but Nelly wasn't really listening because she was looking up at the airship heading away, with her own balloon following

after, like a calf. And after a while the boy stopped talking and watched too. They watched together until the specks were out of sight, and then he picked up where he had started.

'I said left.'

'Fine, you said left.'

And they glared at each other, until Nelly asked him what he had tattooed on his arm, and he became more cheerful.

'Broccoli,' he said, rolling up his sleeve, and explained that he had done it himself with a needle and green ink.

'Keep your enemies close,' he advised.

Which made her laugh.

'I'm Nelly Peabody,' she said, holding out her hand.

'I'm Ben,' said the boy on the buoy and shook it.

It took a little while for Nelly to forgive Ben for not being the person she had wanted him to be, but it was hard to stay angry for long, because he had such an interesting way of talking, and once he had started, he didn't stop: about broccoli, about vegetables, about the disgusting things that live in the ocean, such as plankton.

'What are plankton?'

'Tiny creatures too small to see. Whales eat them. Also my grandfather. He makes them into soup, and let me tell you that plankton soup is even more disgusting than broccoli soup.'

'What does it taste like?'

'Try some. The water round here is stiff with the stuff. Just lower a bucket.'

'Is that why it's red?'

'Yes, and when you eat them, they make everything else red too, just like beetroot. Disgusting! Grandpa serves them twice a day, sometimes three, which is why I'm sitting on this buoy, because I won't eat plankton soup for breakfast.'

'But where's your grandfather?'

'In the doldrums, I should think. He's a great sulker. But he should be back to pick us up once he's cooled off, in a day or two.'

'But isn't that him now?'

'Where?'

And Nelly pointed to a sail that had

appeared on the horizon.

'That's not my grandfather,' said Ben, running over to the rail to get a better look. 'That's my mother's ship! *The Bell-Hammer.*'

The Bell-Hammer was the kind of ship you get in fairy tales, with green flags flying from its masts and an angel figurehead at its prow. With sails the colour of autumn leaves, yellow, red, and orange, all stacked up on top of each other. It came towards them like fire on the water, but it wasn't alone. When Nelly got out her telescope, she saw two more ships on either side of it, their sails the same colour as the haze on the horizon: a soft, funereal grey.

'Smugglers!' exclaimed Ben, sucking in his breath.

'Are they after her?' asked Nelly.

'Not likely,' he grinned, and explained

that his mother was a sea ranger, a righteous terror in every corner of the world, known in some parts as Bloody Barbara, in others as Salt Barbara, and others still as Hairy Barbara, on account of her war wigs.

'That's *The Bell-Hammer*. The fastest, most feared ship on the ocean. It'll be her who's chasing them, you'll see.'

'Is she some sort of pirate?'

'Mother? No! She eats pirates for breakfast. But she hates smugglers worse.'

'What's a war wig?'

'A wig to go to war in. Mother shaves the heads of her enemies and uses the cuttings.'

'Are they comfortable?'

'How should I know? She's never let me try one on. She never lets me do anything. Why do you think I'm stuck with Grandpa while she has all the fun?'

'Is he really so bad?'

'Far worse than you can imagine. The plankton's actually the least of it; there's also algebra and family history, not to mention a weekly test on the rules and regulations of the ship; although you never call a submarine a ship, apparently. You have to call it a boat.'

'Your grandfather lives aboard a submarine?'

'That's what I said,' said Ben.

'Why?'

'Because he's a submarine admiral, I suppose, and that's what submarine admirals do. In the old days the whole family used to live down there with him, and they'd all float about together. But now they've left and he lives there on his own, like a solitary sardine in a rusty sardine can —unless of course I'm with him, in which case, make that two sardines.'

'Doesn't he get sad?'

'I should think so. There's no floating about any more. Nothing interesting ever happens. He just parks his rust bucket at the bottom of the ocean, right beneath this old buoy, and whoever has to stay down there with him had better bring a book.'

'Doesn't he ever come up for air?'

'Only to dump me on it or to collect his mail.'

'Poor thing!' said Nelly.

'He is not a poor thing. He's a monster.'

But before Ben could say another word, the conversation was interrupted by a series of bangs, like corn popping in a pan, and looking up Nelly saw that *The Bell-Hammer* and the two grey ships were almost upon them, with all guns blazing.

CHAPTER

ELEVEN

The Bell-Hammer flew towards them like a torch, with the smuggler ships to port and starboard, slender as greyhounds; ships built for speed, with grey hulls and grey sails, skimming over the water as the smoke of their cannons poured from their sides.

'BANG!' went the guns, and when Nelly fetched her telescope from her duffel bag, she could see figures running to and fro with buckets to put out fires; climbing up the rigging to replace torn canvas; bending low over the mouths of cannon with long sticks to pack in the gunpowder.

'Let me have a go!' shouted Ben, and Nelly handed him the telescope, because now the ships were so close she could see everything that was happening with her naked eye. The smugglers to left and right, and on the deck of *The Bell-Hammer*, towering above her crew, a tall figure in glittering armour: Ben's mother shouting orders, with a war wig on her head like a lick of red flame.

It was such a beautiful sight that Nelly did not want to lose a second of it. She just stood with her mouth open as Hairy Barbara directed the business of war with a pistol in one hand and a cutlass in the other. Closer came the ships. Closer and closer, until Nelly could almost hear the captain's orders as she was giving them.

'What's she saying?' she asked Ben, who was still peering through the telescope.

'Who?'

'Your mother.'

'She's telling us to jump.'

'Jump!' shouted Barbara. 'JUMP!'

But by the time Nelly and Ben realized what was happening, it was too late, because the first smuggler ship was already upon them.

'BOOM!' went its guns, and a cannonball came skipping towards them across the water, then bounded lazily over their heads, so close Nelly could hear it sizzle.

For a second she could see the smugglers themselves, their grey hair blowing in the wind, staring at her over the gunwales. And then their ship sped by: a boat the colour of driftwood, seeming to float a little above the water, disappearing towards the opposite horizon while a hundred yards away Ben's mother's ship stood its ground as the second smuggler ship bore down.

'Why doesn't she fire back?' shouted Nelly.

'She's afraid of hitting us.'

But Ben and Nelly couldn't move. They stood where they were, paralysed by the terror of it: the guns, the smoke, the noise—the almost certain outcome. But then the smuggler ship faltered, as if it had taken an invisible blow.

'Torpedo!' shouted Ben, his face white with excitement.

And as they watched, the grey ship came to pieces. One moment it had been standing tall, its grey sails drinking in the wind; the next, it was broken, heeling over on its side, letting in the sea—its nose already lifting as its crew tumbled over the shattered gunwales.

And then, as Nelly watched, the crimson water began to boil.

'What's happening?'

'It's Grandpa!' shouted Ben, punching the air, 'He's coming up!'

And up Ben's grandpa came: a monster from the deep, but not a giant octopus or angry titan woken from a ten-thousand-year slumber. A colossal man-made monster, covered in barnacles and strands of seaweed and curious white scars, with its name written in green letters on its bow: *The Kraken*.

With a squeak of rusty hinges, a round hatch opened on top of the submarine's tower, and out of it came the torso of a man with a moustache wider than his shoulders and a voice like the bellow of a bull walrus signalling the end of time.

'What's going on here?' he roared, staring about him furiously, so that his eyebrows stuck out like accusing fingers, first at Barbara aboard *The Bell-Hammer*, then at the smugglers floating in the water (clinging to the remaining bits and pieces of their ship), then at Nelly and Ben where they stood on their buoy. But nobody seemed inclined to speak so Nelly thought she'd better introduce herself.

'There's been a battle,' she said, 'but it's over now. This is Ben, although of course you know that already, and that's your daughter, Barbara. I'm Nelly—pleased to meet you—and this is my turtle, Columbus, although don't expect him to shake hands. He's had a bit of a shock.'

THE KRAKEN.

CHAPTER TWELVE

Once the prisoners had been scooped out of the water and the Admiral and Barbara had joined them on the buoy, Nelly explained who she was, and where she had come from. But the Admiral did not reply. For a moment, he stood speechless, his eyes popping beneath his eyebrows, and when he spoke, it was in a hoarse whisper.

'Nelly?' he said, 'Nelly Peabody?'

'That's right.'

'Daughter of Penelope?'

'Penelope Peabody, yes.'

'And that utter scoundrel Captain Bones Peabody of the so-called Gentlemen's Exploratory Flotilla?'

'My father is not a scoundrel!' objected Nelly, hotly. 'He is an explorer.'

'Same thing,' growled the old man.

'It is not the same!'

'It is.'

'No it's not.'

'No,' agreed Barbara, 'it isn't the same at all. Pirates are scoundrels. Smugglers are scoundrels. Explorers can go either way, and I for one am prepared to give Captain Bones the benefit of the doubt, since his wife is my sister, which makes this young lady my niece.'

At which Barbara took Nelly's hand and said she was delighted to make her acquaintance, and that anybody, even a fool, would be proud to have her as a relative.

'And I am proud!' said the Admiral, blushing so that his moustache and eyebrows shone a snowy white. 'Very!'

'You see?' smiled Barbara, 'your grandfather is proud. But now I have to go, because there's work to do.'

And she pointed to the horizon, where the second smuggler ship was busy making its escape.

'Take me with you!' begged Ben.

'When you're older.'

'I'll be good. I'll eat my greens.'

'Stay until I'm done.'

'You can't make me!' shouted Ben, clenching his fists and staring up at his mother, who was six-and-a-half feet tall in her boots and over seven in her war-wig; a towering

giantess with pistols in her belt and a cutlass by her side, wearing a dazzling coat of mail. A warrior queen who could have made anybody do anything she wanted, still grimy from the smog of battle. But she only smiled and kissed her son on the forehead, then kissed Nelly too before she waved goodbye.

'There goes Aunt Barbara,' whispered Nelly to Columbus, as the golden sails disappeared into the distance.

'I hope she rots in hell,' said Ben, shaking his fist.

'Take that back,' roared the Admiral.

'I will not.'

'You will.'

'I will not.'

'You'll do what you're told and like it!'

'Or what?'

'Or I'll clap you in irons with these rascals.'

And Nelly's grandfather gestured at the prisoners who stood dripping nearby, pressing close together for safety, with their long grey beards hanging from hollow cheeks and their rusty pistols and cutlasses lying before them in a pile.

'Then clap me in irons!' shouted Ben, not at all daunted.

So, once everybody was safely aboard, the Admiral clapped his grandson in irons, along with the smugglers, then sounded the klaxon that meant *The Kraken* was ready to dive.

CHAPTER
THIRTEEN

Nelly had never had a grandfather before and at first she was shy of him, because of his moustache and the gold buttons on his jacket, and the stripes on his sleeves which showed how important he was. There was so much gold at his shoulders, she thought of birds with gorgeous feathers, bright eyes, and sharp beaks; except she had never seen a bird with so many medals, or any medals at all, and the Admiral had dozens of them. Some were round and some were shaped like crosses, and they hung from his chest on coloured ribbons—red, green, and blue.

But she didn't stay shy for long, because he was so obviously delighted to see her, and the moment *The Kraken* had begun its dive, asked her to tell her story properly from the beginning. So Nelly told him, trying not to leave out any of the important bits. About the trip to the North Pole and coming home to find her mother gone, and the retired cabin boy sitting in her chair.

'Wearing her slippers you say?'

'And knitting with her knitting needles.'

'Preposterous!'

In fact, Nelly found her grandfather a very agreeable audience in almost every way. When she told him about the storm, he gripped the arms of his chair until his knuckles cracked. When she told him about the wind map, and the blob she had mistaken for strawberry jam, he laughed, and listened to her account of the man dangling in mid-air beneath the airship so intently that she thought perhaps he didn't believe her—then turned white when she told him what it was like to jump out of a hot-air balloon at twenty thousand feet.

'Beneath a woollen blanket?'

'That's right.'

'You don't mean it!'

'I do. It really happened. Ask Ben.'

'Extraordinary!'

And he showed her the depth gauge (which is just another kind of barometer) which measured the depth to which they had already sunk beneath the surface of the sea, simply by weighing it.

'Five hundred fathoms,' he said, 'and falling.'

'How many fathoms is it to the bottom?' asked Nelly, thinking of the water already above their heads.

'About six thousand—or seven miles, if you want to think of it another way.'

'Seven miles?' said Nelly. 'Isn't that very deep indeed?'

'It's the deepest place on Earth,' replied the Admiral, with relish, and offered to take her on a tour of the boat.

The Kraken was a military submarine, and visitors were expected to keep military discipline, whatever personal views they might have on the matter. No boots were worn on deck because the sound of footsteps carried a long way underwater, so the Admiral went about in socks. There were no bright lights, either, or portholes, because no glass was strong enough to withstand the immense weight of water pressing in. Only iron would do the trick, which was why everything aboard *The Kraken* was made of the stuff. It was like a dimly-lit iron bottle full of air, with each room shut off from the next by a door that could be locked by spinning a wheel. A room full of guns and swords. A room full of trophies. An entire room filled with diving suits—the family diving suits—going back to the days when Porbeagles walked along the floor of the ocean wearing nothing but buckets on their heads.

'What's a Porbeagle?' asked Nelly.

'What's a Porbeagle?' said her grandfather, looking hurt. 'You're a Porbeagle. I'm a Porbeagle. We're all Porbeagles. It's the family name.'

'But I'm a Peabody!' said Nelly.

'You were a Porbeagle first,' said the Admiral savagely, and he took her to the maps room to show her the family tree, with its top branches in the clouds and its roots snaking along the ocean floor—*The Kraken* nestling amongst them.

'That's us,' he said, pointing to a branch very close to the bottom, and taking a gold pen from his pocket, he wrote Nelly's name next to Ben's.

'First cousins,' he explained, putting the top back on.

'Do you have a crew?' asked Nelly, who hadn't seen a single other person apart from her grandfather since they had locked Ben and the smugglers away in the scuppers.

'Not if I can help it,' said the Admiral, and he showed her his cabin, which was so small he could reach anything he needed from the bunk: his wardrobe, his sink, his lavatory, which was a wooden box with the family crest—a Porbeagle shark—carved on the lid. Everything so crisp and tidy Nelly was afraid to turn around, so she stood poker-straight in the middle with her arms by her sides.

'Where's Granny?' she asked, noticing a nightdress hanging from the back of the door.

'Swallowed by an avalanche,' he said, looking so sad Nelly wished she hadn't asked. 'All they found were her boots.'

And before he could explain any further, or change the subject, the klaxon sounded for supper.

That evening, Nelly had a wash in the Porbeagle family bath, which stood on bronze walruses and had taps shaped like fishes. Then she ate supper in the dining room, which was lined with family portraits, while the Admiral sieved plankton soup through his moustache (very much as whales do) and told her about her ancestors. Her great-great-grandmother Scott who founded the post office. Her great-great-grandfather Porbeagle who laid the first telegraphic cable to Australia. Her grandmother, Clare Scott, who was one of

the three original founders of the Fiennes, Hilary, and Scott catalogue.

'Granny founded the Fiennes, Hilary, and Scott catalogue?'

'She gave her life to it,' said the Admiral, and he told Nelly how his wife had vanished crossing the Himalayas at the head of a mule train.

'Do you think Mother might have gone looking for her?'

And Nelly reminded him of the note in the cabin boy's pocket: 'Gone to visit Granny, back soon.'

'Penelope? In the Himalayas? It's an awfully long way.'

'But all the same, she might have done.'

Nelly stirred her soup, which was not very appetizing.

'She might be there right now. She might be wandering around on her own, looking for Granny, without anybody to help her.'

'I doubt it.'

'But don't you think we should go and see?'

'How do you mean?' said the Admiral, shooting her a glance from under his eyebrows.

'I mean, don't you think we should send out a search party?'

At which his mood suddenly altered.

'Think?' he demanded, '*Think*? What is there to think about? Here is my granddaughter, a small girl who has stepped down from a hot-air balloon, using only a woollen blanket as a parachute. Where is her mother? God knows! Where is her father? Chasing butterflies at the North Pole! And who is looking after this girl? Nobody, that's who! Unless you count one medium-sized turtle with his head in his shell—yes, I am talking about you, sir!'

And he jabbed his finger at Columbus.

'But all the same,' said Nelly.

'Nobody is sending out any search parties!' roared the Admiral. 'Nobody is going on any more adventures! Nobody is leaving this submarine until I say so, and I say that small girls do not float about the world in hot-air balloons looking for their mothers, or sail about in ships looking for their fathers. They have a hot bath and eat supper with their grandfathers. This grandfather here! And then they go to bed and get a good night's sleep, because in the morning they will be tested on the rules and regulations that keep this boat from becoming a madhouse! Do I make myself clear?'

'Perfectly,' said Nelly, and was about to tell him what she thought of him, grandfather or not, when there was a thump that sent a tremor through the whole submarine.

'What was that?' she said, hugging her turtle to her chest.

'That,' said the Admiral, grimly, 'was the sound of *The Kraken* hitting the bottom.'

CHAPTER FOURTEEN

Nelly spent that night at the bottom of the Challenger Deep, which as the Admiral had already pointed out, is the deepest place on Earth, shut away in her mother's room, which had not been touched since Penelope left the boat to marry Captain Peabody. It was not exactly a comfortable room, but neither was it a dungeon. Against one wall was a wardrobe, against the other, a four-poster bed, and against a third, a desk. An iron room Nelly found so familiar that for a moment she wondered if she might have visited before, until she remembered that Columbus had shown it to her in a dream, right at the beginning of the adventure. The dream in which she had seen Penelope as a girl about her own age, writing at the desk, and afterwards hiding a key. And when Nelly lifted one of the carved wooden acorns that topped the bedposts, there it was, just where she had expected. A key that fitted a locked drawer containing Penelope's secret diary.

Nelly had never read somebody else's diary before—their private thoughts and feelings—and as she passed by the mirror on the wardrobe, she could not help apologizing to her own reflection.

'I'm sorry.'

She hesitated again when she lay down on the bed and opened it to the first page, where Penelope had written a terrible warning in thick felt-tip pen:

HANDS OFF BARBARA, THIS IS NONE OF YOUR BUSINESS!!

But she read it anyway, because it belonged to her mother, and because (in a way) Columbus had told her to—and in any case, very soon she was too interested to remember she was doing anything wrong.

'Fire drill.'

'Barbara angry.'

'Mama came to visit.'

At the beginning, the writing was large and round, and the drawings were not very good: a starfish; something that might have been a sea anemone. But every now and then there would be a break, as if Penelope had grown bored or forgotten to keep it for a while.

'Nanny broke a plate.'

'Nanny lost at cards.'

'Nanny taught me how to do the crossword puzzle. Also knitting.'

Now and then the Admiral would make an appearance, but generally it was Nanny or Barbara, or Nanny and Barbara, or just Penelope on her own, thinking her own thoughts. Often sad thoughts because it is lonely growing up aboard a submarine, without much to do or many people to talk to. With no garden to walk in or trees to climb or windows to look out of, or even a sea to swim in, because most of the time *The Kraken* was under water and the lights were turned down low.

'Played patience.'

Occasionally Penelope would talk about somebody called Marina, making Nelly wonder if maybe there was a third sister, until she came across a picture of Marina in the bath, with her mermaid fish's tail adjusting the taps—an imaginary friend. Nelly wasn't surprised, because she would probably have done the same thing herself if she had not got Columbus to keep her company. But Penelope had no real friends. In fact the only thing she really looked forward to was her mother visiting. A mother who was usually absent, gone for months and months at a time on business of her own. Fiennes, Hilary, and Scott business. And then she would come back and Penelope would describe the places she had been: mountains, rivers, forests, deserts; camel trains, and mule trains, and log rafts loaded with cargo.

'Mama bought a new ship.'

'Mama gave me a four-leafed clover.'

'Mama took me to the new storeroom,'

accompanied by a very
skilful picture of a
vaulted treasure house,
done with glitter and
paints on a piece of
paper that folded out to
do the spectacle justice.

'Mama off climbing.'

And then shortly after Penelope's
sixteenth birthday, one word: 'Mama.'

And that was that. No more Mama. Just
a lonely girl growing up underwater, doing
her school work, arguing with her sister,
waiting for something. Until, at the back of
the diary, Nelly found an unfinished letter,
which she did not read, because it was a
love letter.

'Darling Bones . . .'

Nelly lay on the bed with Columbus

101

beside her, and when she had finished reading, she thought of *The Sky Lantern* floating somewhere high above, airy and free, then again of how deep down she was: the balloon and the submarine on the front of Penelope's diary. She imagined her mother lying where she now lay, locked in an iron room at the bottom of the ocean, and as she drifted off to sleep she felt the water pressing in on her, hugging her tight like a lonely monster. A creature of the deep, with huge eyes and tentacles, wrapping itself around her—until she was startled by a knock on the door, and jumping out of bed found Ben, standing in the corridor swinging a bunch of keys and grinning from ear to ear.

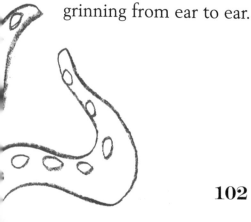

'Are you pleased to see me?'

'Yes,' said Nelly.

And she was—very.

'Good,' said Ben, 'because I've brought some new friends.'

And into the room, one after another, came the smugglers.

CHAPTER
FIFTEEN

Ben's new friends arranged themselves around the room like soft, bare-footed shadows. Some sat on Penelope's bed or stood by the bedposts. Others leaned against the wardrobe or the desk (one

sat on the chair). They wore grey woolly jumpers and soft grey trousers, and it was hard to tell the difference between them unless Nelly looked very closely—at their fingers or their noses, or at the colour of their beards, which were sometimes lighter and sometimes darker than their skin. Otherwise, they were the same, with eyes set in deep grey sockets, glittering as Ben explained his plan. How he was fed up with

being a prisoner aboard his grandfather's submarine and had decided to become a smuggler himself.

'It all came to me when I was clapped in irons—what a lot of fun it would be. Sailing around the world without anybody to tell me what to do; except of course that a smuggler needs a ship, just like anybody else. But then I thought, wait! I'm sitting in one—the finest smuggler ship there could possibly be. So I decided to stage a mutiny.'

'With your friends?'

'Yes, with my new friends,' he jingled his keys, 'they'll be my crew.'

'But won't the Admiral be angry?'

'Let him be angry! We'll lock him in his cabin and feed him plankton soup through the keyhole until we find a suitable desert island to drop him on.'

He grinned again and the smugglers grinned too. Smiles that showed their teeth, which were not very tidy.

'Are you with us?'

But Nelly wasn't sure, because although it was true the Admiral was bad-tempered, he was also kind. And in any case, what if Ben's new friends turned out not to be so friendly after all? What if one mutiny wasn't enough? What would happen if there were two?

'Do I have any choice?'

At which the smuggler sitting at the desk got to his feet and made a low bow.

'My lady,' he said, in a voice as soft as cobwebs, 'we were sailing home when our ship was attacked, and now, perhaps, we have a new one. But we do not mean to hurt you, or the old man. Our laws forbid it. We make war only in self-defence. We do not hurt innocent people. And besides, we have been looking for you.'

'Why?'

'Only our master knows,' shrugged the smuggler, 'but we have been searching a long time, and we are not alone. The Abuela has many ships. But perhaps we would not have succeeded if ours had not been lost. We had not expected to find you at the bottom of the ocean. You and your famous turtle.'

'Well here we are,' said Nelly.

'And we also.'

'And me too!' said Ben. 'Isn't it brilliant?'

'But how can you turn smuggler? What about your mother?'

'That's the best bit!' he said, widening his eyes and rubbing his hands. 'She'll be furious! And if she ever crosses my path, she'd better watch out.'

'You'd torpedo *The Bell-Hammer*?'

'Certainly!'

'And abandon the Admiral on a desert island?'

'With pleasure!'

'And would you let him?' Nelly asked the smuggler.

'I?' he replied. 'I cannot say. The boy is angry with his mother. He does not like his grandfather's soup. So let him do as he wishes. But if the boy wishes to become a smuggler, he must give up his family and take another name, such as The Prawn, perhaps, or The Little Pig. He must obey our laws, and then he will not be angry any more, because he will not be the same person. He will be one of us and live as we do, beneath the Abuela.'

'The Abuela?'

'The Abuela who is our master. It means "Granny".'

CHAPTER SIXTEEN

It wasn't difficult to hijack *The Kraken* once the decision had been made to do it. First Ben locked the Admiral (still snoring) safely in his room. Then he unlocked the door to the armoury, where the smugglers retrieved their rusty pistols and cutlasses, thrusting them into their belts with little grunts and puffs of satisfaction. Finally he led the way to the control room, where he pulled the necessary levers that lifted *The Kraken* off the ocean floor and sent it sailing up again towards the surface.

'There's nothing to it really,' Ben admitted, as the smugglers wandered off to explore the boat. 'It's like a gigantic airship.'

'But where are we going?'

'To visit the Abuela, of course—in his

110

secret headquarters. They call it the Devil's Ballroom.'

And he told her the legends that surrounded the smuggler-in-chief's hidden fortress. The ghosts and monsters that guarded its doorways. The wonderful treasure inside, filling caves that stretched for miles, some beneath the water, some above: a warren only half discovered by the smugglers who lived there.

'How do you know so much about it?'

'Mother told me—the bit about the ghosts and the treasure, anyway. Some people say it's filled with the souls of the dead, and that the Devil dances with them every night. Others that the Abuela actually is the devil, and can take whatever shape he likes: an old woman, a man, a horse, a dog. They say that when he's in a bad mood the caves are full of roaring and screaming, and when he's happy, there's lovely music instead. But the smugglers say that's all nonsense, and that the Abuela is just a man like anybody else. Apparently something terrible happened to him that made him very wise and kind, although he does seem to get a bit angry sometimes—or at least his smugglers seem very relieved to have found you. And now we're all going to visit him in his headquarters!'

Ben paused to relish the thought of it.

'My mother's been hunting him for years and years but she's never actually met him. She's never seen his lair. But we will, you and me—and then we'll join his fleet and become smugglers too, and there's nothing she or Grandpa can do about it. Just let them try!'

The first time the klaxon sounded for breakfast, it woke the Admiral, who raved and threatened to knock down his door (an iron door four inches thick), until Ben explained—with a wink to Nelly— that *The Kraken* had been hijacked by the smugglers and he and his cousin were being held hostage.

'If you behave,' he said, 'they'll set us free. If not we'll be thrown to the sharks.'

So the Admiral behaved, on condition that his grandchildren presented themselves every two hours at his keyhole to prove they were safe and sound. Which they did, delivering meals three times a day and occasionally stopping to chat, although there were subjects Nelly found it wise to avoid.

'He doesn't seem to like my father very much,' she told Ben.

'Nor mine.'

'Is yours an explorer too?'

'He's an aeronaut. I thought you met him. You were talking to him just before you jumped out of your balloon.'

'So that's why you were waving!'

'Why else?'

'I thought you were waving at me,' Nelly blushed. 'I thought you were my mother.'

'And I wanted to be rescued. I thought he might lower a rope!'

'But he lowered Columbus instead,' recalled Nelly, gratefully. 'Tell me about him.'

So Ben told her about his father, Carl, who sailed around the world in his airship, and had the same horror of low places that some people have of heights, a kind of upside-down vertigo. Gentle Carl, who had never spoken a single word—not, at least, in anybody but Barbara's hearing—so that the only reason Ben knew he was called Carl at all was because his mother had told him.

'What does he do up there?'

'I haven't the faintest idea. What does your father do?'

'He's an explorer. He sailed away the day after I was born and discovered a volcano at the North Pole. But he's coming home. He just needs to build himself a new ship.'

'No wonder Grandpa doesn't like him.'

'He would if he met him.'

'I doubt it. In any case, we're smugglers now. Family doesn't matter.'

'I suppose not.'

Although it seemed a shame to Nelly, who was just beginning to discover that she had a family at all—a cousin, an aunt and uncle, a grandfather—to have to give them all up just as she was getting used to the idea.

'Do you suppose Granny's the Abuela?' she wondered

'Granny? How could she be? She's dead.'

'But suppose she isn't. Suppose she's just pretending. Suppose she vanished deliberately and decided to become a smuggler instead?'

'But the Abuela is a he.'

'Then why do they call him Granny?'

'I don't know, you'll have to ask him,' said Ben, a little bitterly, 'since he's so fond of you.'

CHAPTER

SEVENTEEN

How long does it take to travel from the deepest place on Earth to the Devil's front door? Half a day to rise from the Challenger Deep? A week or a month cruising through the open ocean? Except that time does not pass like that in an iron bottle. The rooms Nelly walked through were as dimly lit as ever, however bright the water outside the submarine's iron hull. The hull vibrated with the same dull tremor of its engines. At six o'clock every morning the klaxon sounded for breakfast, and she chatted to the smugglers, or to Ben, or to the Admiral through his keyhole. At night the klaxon went again for supper, and afterwards Nelly went to bed in her mother's room and when she fell asleep dreamed of the

Devil's Ballroom, or the Abuela, or ghosts of the past that might have followed *The Kraken* up from the absolute deep, taking the form of monstrous worms or jellyfish.

Then the klaxon would sound again for breakfast—'OO-Whaahh!!'—and the whole thing started over again, round and round. Until one day, long after Nelly had stopped counting the days, the lights flickered, the engines slowed, and after checking maps and consulting compasses, somebody announced that they had arrived.

The only difficulty was that Aunt Barbara had arrived too.

'Damn!' swore Ben, looking through the periscope.

And there, floating on the water, was *The Bell-Hammer*, with its green flags and golden sails splendid against a bank of white fog.

'Trust her to spoil our fun.'

'Can we go underneath her?'

'Not unless we want to hit the rocks.'

'Or around?'

'Too shallow.'

In fact Aunt Barbara sat on top of the harbour's only navigable channel.

'Is there really no other way?' asked Nelly.

'There's a back door,' said a smuggler.

'But it is very small,' said another.

'Like a mouse hole,' added a third, making a tiny hole with his finger and thumb. 'Much too narrow for a big boat like this to pass through.'

'Well that settles it,' said Ben, 'we'll just have to torpedo her.'

'You wouldn't!' said Nelly.

'I would!'

'I won't let you!'

'Just try to stop me!'

And they went back and forth like that until Nelly drew her red-handled cutlass and Ben his rusty one. Nobody tried to get in the way. Nobody said a word. The smugglers just watched as the cousins dared one another to do whatever they were going to do; and perhaps they would actually have done it if somebody—or something—had not intervened.

CLICKETY-CLACK

'CRASH!'

'CRUNCH!'

First a bump, then a lurch, as the boat heeled over, like a barrel rolling in the water.

'BANG!'

Then the other way, throwing everything that wasn't screwed down tumbling end over end.

'PING!'

'PRRRANGGG!'

'What was that?' shouted Nelly.

But nobody answered, because they couldn't hear her over the din. Doors swinging open and slamming shut. Iron plates groaning and booming as they buckled. Sounds like gunshots as iron rivets shot free of their sockets—water hissing in through the gaps. The whole frame of the submarine being crumpled out of shape as whatever had it in its grip shook it up and down like a tin can.

'Make for the diving room!' shouted the Admiral, as the door of his cabin was torn from its hinges. 'Follow me!'

And his walrus bellow was so powerful that nobody could fail to hear him.

'Seal the door!' he yelled, when they were all inside, and as Nelly spun the wheel, he was already cramming Ben into one of the Porbeagle family diving suits, then Nelly, and finally himself, tightening the bolts around his helmet as the water lapped beneath his chin.

Nelly didn't panic, although she was very frightened indeed. She did what she had to do, although she did not understand what was happening. But then she realized she couldn't see Columbus, and began to scream.

'There's no time!' shouted the Admiral, as she tried (idiotically) to take her own helmet off again.

'There's no *time!*'

122

And Nelly was falling, somersaulting into the open ocean as the weight of her suit— iron and brass and galvanized rubber— dragged her down, and suddenly there was plenty of time for everything. Time to count the suited bodies falling with her. Time to look up at *The Kraken* being torn to pieces, gripped by a monster with rolling eyes and snake-like arms that felt for any stray pieces that might have escaped its attention— tables, smashed-up chairs, human beings. Time to feel one of its tentacles coil around her own waist and then let go as somebody stabbed at it with a cutlass.

Nelly had time to notice everything, but she could do nothing about it. She fell inside her suit, looking out through the round window in her helmet, and saw what she saw, then felt the soft thud as she hit the sandy floor of the ocean, where rough hands picked her up and carried her to the mouth of a cave—an opening so small she could barely squeeze inside.

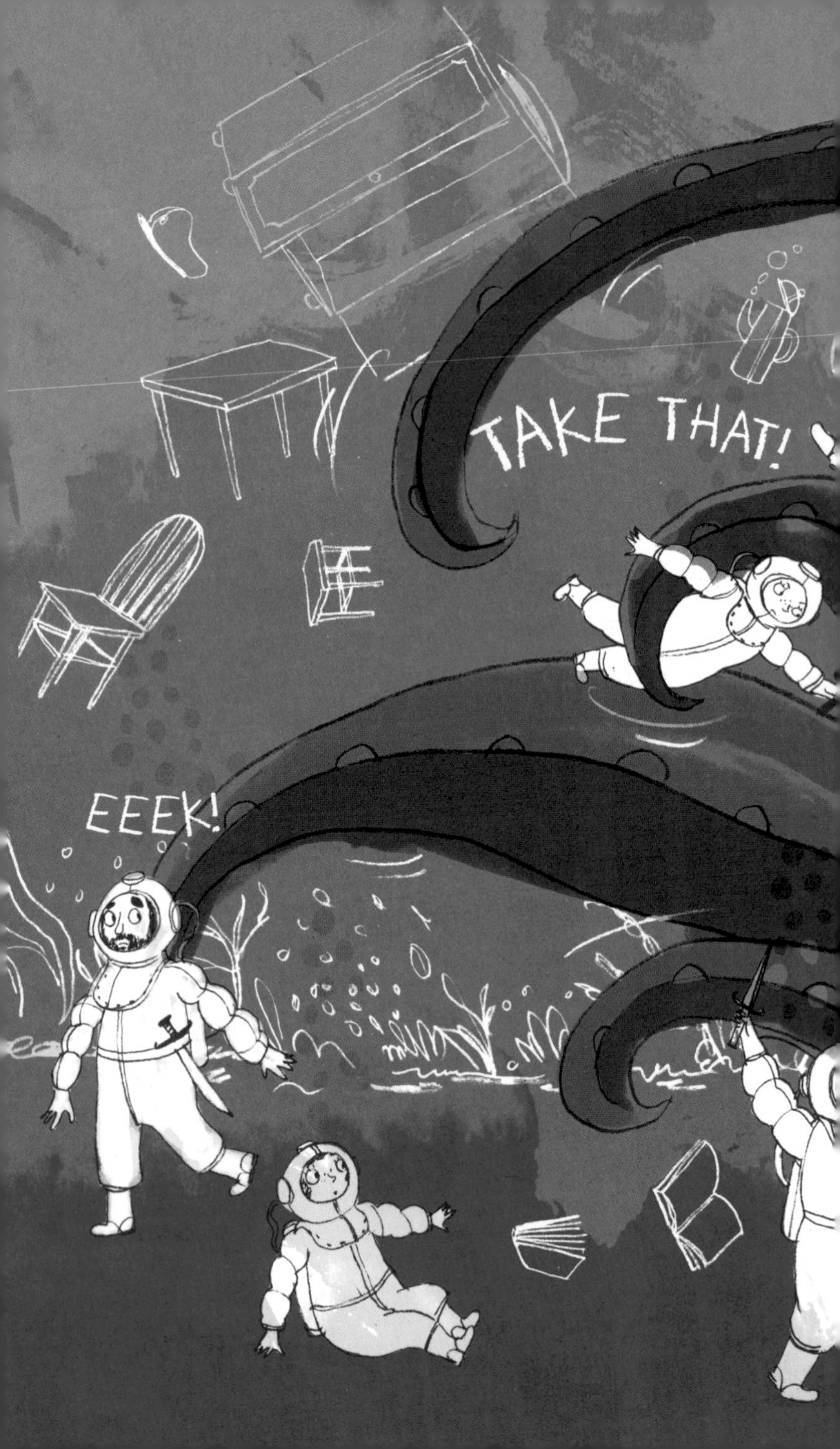
TAKE THAT!
EEEK!

EIGHTEEN

If Nelly had not felt Columbus close by, she would not have been able to go on, but she did feel him. She couldn't see him, because it was dark, but she knew he was there, telling her it was all right, because water is nothing to be frightened of. Not for a turtle. Much better to be deep down in the ocean than miles up in the air, bobbing about beneath a balloon, and far better to be in a cave than an iron bottle. A nice dark cave, like a shell for Nelly to pull her head into, because outside something frightening was still thrashing about in the water. Something that had followed *The Kraken* up from the deep because it did not want to let it go.

Nelly, of course, was not a turtle.

Her boots were very heavy. The iron breastplate and helmet weighed her down. She kept knocking her head against the ceiling and tripping on rocks, banging her knees and elbows. Trapped inside her suit, she breathed ancient Porbeagle air through a tube. If she damaged the iron tanks on her back, she knew she would die. If she tore a hole in the canvas skin of the suit, she would also die. All around her the water pressed in, and the dark too, but Columbus was with her. He told her that everything was all right because they were in a good place: the very best sort of place. And although she couldn't see him or touch him, she knew he was there in the water beside her, or closer. Columbus who had always been her friend. Who had arrived on her first birthday, still in his egg, in a cake tin full of sand (along with a shoebox full of snails), and had been with her ever since. Dear, wise Columbus, like a warm thread pulling her through the dark—miles of it—as the stale air in her tank thinned. Keeping her alive until she stumbled out of the tunnel and fell forwards onto a stone floor.

'Where's my turtle?' she gasped, as soon as the bolts of her helmet were loosened.

'I'm sorry,' said a voice like cobwebs, 'he is not here.'

There was no sign of Ben or the Admiral either. Only Nelly and a handful of smugglers and a black circle of water behind them.

The smugglers wouldn't let Nelly sit where she was, although she wanted to. At first they carried her, still in her suit. When she stopped kicking, they put her down. They told her Columbus was a turtle and she should not worry about him; he would have found another way around.

'But I heard him,' said Nelly, 'in the water.'

'So you see he is fine. He has found another way, but we have only one. Come!'

And they led her on, first down a tunnel lined with torches, then through a low arch, out into a cave that would have been beautiful if Nelly had noticed it, then another and another. Now and then her

boots would crunch over mussel shells or razor clams, or slip on something oozy—a bed of seaweed, a sponge—and she would steady herself against a wall soft with moss. Then she would plod on after the smugglers, grey figures moving through the torch-lit gloom, which widened and brightened as the torches became more numerous. Hundreds of torches burning low to the ground, then climbing in zigzags, lining paths and stairways. The Abuela's underground kingdom—the Devil's Ballroom—not silent but filled with the roar and hiss of waves and the nearby drip of water, echoing in the hollow space and making Nelly's ears ring.

Nelly walked for a long time before she noticed that the light was not always torchlight. Up in the roof, there were narrow chimneys, and down them wormed a weak sort of daylight, falling through the air in shafts criss-crossed by bats on the wing—tiny bodies swirling and squeaking. After a while, the floor was soft with their droppings, or brittle with their tiny skeletons, but further on it was swept clean, and the ceilings were higher. Caves lined with treasure, but not gold or precious gems. Instead, wooden chests filled with coffee or cocoa, jars of nutmeg and turmeric. In one chamber, spices; in another, rolls of cloth. One cave was strung across with ropes like washing lines hung with salami sausage and hams. Another was full of cheese, and even Nelly could not help being impressed. A cheese cave fifty feet high, with wooden shelves going all the way up to the ceiling, lined with great yellow rounds of cheese smelling so strongly they made her dizzy.

'And does the Devil really live here?' she asked, holding her nose.

'Come and see,' said the smugglers, and they led her on, through caverns filled with leather and others with jars of buttons,

and one like a massive
stone wardrobe
hung with dresses.
Astonishing dresses in
every colour and fabric,
hung from a
wall studded with
nubs of stone to make
a ladder, and beneath
them row after row
of boots and shoes.

But the smugglers
wouldn't let Nelly
dawdle. They led her on
across a rickety bridge
made of slats of wood
held together with
string, then another
made only of rope.

'If I were to jump
now,' Nelly thought,
'that would be the end.'

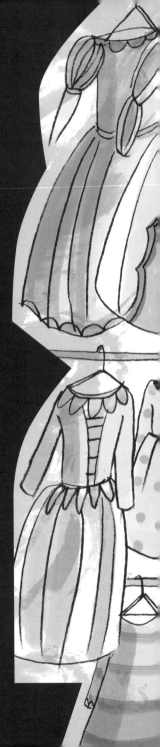

But something told her not to jump—a friendly voice inside her—although once she nearly fell, because her diving boots were not the sort of slippers she would have chosen for a high wire act.

Finally, she squeezed through a narrow door and came out into a room shaped like a huge stone bottle, with stairs spiralling up the wall, narrowing to a chimney that let down a yellowish light. A sad, ill sort of light that showed her the sandy floor, and in the middle of the room, a small house: a hut built of twigs and planks of driftwood, with

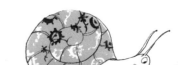

empty windows and a
rickety door.

'Master,' said the
cobwebs, 'may we
come in?'

'Yes, yes,' called

a voice.

And when Nelly walked inside, there, seated at a low table was the retired cabin boy.

CHAPTER
NINETEEN

Nelly had never been so surprised to see anybody in her life. The retired cabin boy she had hired from the Fiennes, Hilary, and Scott catalogue to look after her mother while she was away, large as life, with his feet still stuck in her mother's slippers— although he wasn't wearing Captain Peabody's dressing gown any more. He was stripped to the waist like a pirate captain, sweating in the steam that rose from a nearby kettle, and covered in tattoos. On one arm, a dozen ships of various shapes and sizes. On the other an anchor with MUM written underneath it. Around the wrist of his right hand he had S-T-A-R-B-O-A-R-D, like a bracelet, and around his left, P-O-R-T, done in green and red

136

respectively to match a ship's side lights. Otherwise (aside from the pistols thrust into his belt) he was the same, with grey hair made yellow by the light that filtered down through the roof and in through the empty windows. With blue eyes and uneven teeth.

'Cup of tea?' he asked, gesturing to the kettle.

'What are you doing here?' asked Nelly, warily.

'What am I doing? This is my home. This is where I live.'

'In this cave? With the smugglers?'

'Yes.'

'But you're not the Abuela?'

'Oh yes. Yes I am. That's what they call me, at any rate, and I don't mind. It means Granny.'

'But you're not a granny.'

'No,' said the retired cabin boy. 'Not in the usual sense. In fact I have no family at all, unless I count yours.'

And as he turned to make the tea, she saw another tattoo, covering his back. The Porbeagle family tree, just as she had seen it aboard *The Kraken*—except that Nelly's name was missing.

'Who are you?'

'Me?' said the cabin boy, putting the steaming mugs down on the table between them, 'I'm your mother's nanny, dear.'

And he burst into tears.

When Nelly had read her mother's diary aboard *The Kraken*, she had come across a nanny on almost every page. Nanny reading stories. Nanny making cakes. Nanny teaching her darling Penelope how to knit, or dance, or draw with coloured crayons. When it came to practical matters, such as submarine navigation or family history, it had been the Admiral who set the homework, but it had been Nanny who helped Penelope do it, just as it had been Nanny who comforted Penelope and Barbara after their mother died; who mended their clothes and stuck on plasters and sung them back to sleep when they had nightmares. A nanny, Nelly had imagined, with kind eyes and a round sort of body, wagging her finger when the children were naughty and rewarding them when they were good. Not a tattooed smuggler-in-chief with pistols in his belt and rusty earrings—although when the cabin boy drew Nelly's attention to the tattoos on his fingers she could not doubt that he was telling the truth. Letters drawn above and below the knuckles, spelling out the names of his charges: on his left hand, B–A–R–B–A–R–A, and P–E–N–E–L–O–P–E on his right.

'Barbara was difficult,' he sniffed. 'Very headstrong. But your mother was an angel —or everybody thought so, until your grandmother disappeared and she fell in love with an orphan.'

'What sort of orphan?'

'Your father—a young sea captain, without any family of his own. And when Penelope refused to give him up, it made the Admiral so angry, he locked her in her room and wouldn't let her out. He said he'd rather see her starve than let her throw away the Porbeagle family name, and she might have starved if she'd been left to her own devices. She might have pined away to nothing, because Penelope could be headstrong too. But she had a friend.'

'Who?'

'Me,' he grinned, 'her old nanny. In fact, it was at that moment that I first turned smuggler. I carried her letters to your father, and his letters to her, and when she said she wanted to run away with him, I arranged that as well, because I couldn't stand to see her so unhappy. I found them a place to live, and then I went back to *The Kraken* to explain what had happened to your grandfather, because the old man had already lost his wife. I didn't want him to lose his daughter, too, without giving him a chance to say sorry. So back I went, and as a reward, he sacked me on the spot, without any pension. Then he sacked the rest of the crew for good measure and took *The Kraken* down to the deepest, darkest place he could think of, and as far as I know, he's been there ever since.'

'Poor Grandpa!' said Nelly. 'Do you really hate him?'

'See these?' said the cabin boy, pointing to the tattoos on his arm. 'These are all the ships I've served in since you grandfather made a beggar of me. Me, who raised his children and loved them as if they were my own daughters.'

He groaned at the injustice of it.

'But I made friends, Nelly—people like me, who were old and had nothing. We put our pennies together and eventually bought our own ship, and then another, and another. We built a fleet, and I became the man you see now—The Abuela. But I never forgot your mother, or stopped wondering how she was getting on, so when I saw your advert, along I came.'

'But why didn't you tell me all this in the

first place?' asked Nelly.

'Because it was complicated,' said the cabin boy, sipping his tea, so that she could see a branch of the family tree curling under his armpit. 'You see your grandmother was a sort of Abuela herself: the commander-in-chief of The Fiennes, Hilary, and Scott catalogue, which provides explorers with everything they need for the launching of an expedition. And 'everything', Nelly, is a lot of stuff. You need somewhere to put it—a warehouse—but not just any old warehouse: somewhere safe and secret. And, just before she died, your grandmother found just such a place.'

'Right here!' said Nelly, thinking of the treasure house in her mother's diary.

'Right here,' smiled the cabin boy. 'She told me all about it, and when I helped your mother run away, this is where I took her. This is where your parents lived, in these caves. In this very hut, which your father built with his own hands, because at first your mother was afraid of bright light and wide open spaces. The 'downstairs house' they called it. But then you were born and they moved upstairs, and soon after that, your father sailed away.'

'Poor Mama!'

'Yes, poor Mama. She cried and cried, and when I answered your advert, she was still crying, because her daughter had sailed away too. But she was happy to see her old nanny, and when she told me what had happened, I promised to send out my ships to look for you.'

'But you told me she wasn't there! You said the house was empty!'

'I lied.'

'Why?'

'Because I didn't know where she was. You see, when I reminded her about the caves, she went off exploring. She liked it down here, in the dark. She used to talk to the bats as if they were family, and I didn't see any harm in it. I was looking after my own affairs. Until one day she wandered off altogether, leaving nothing but that note.'

'Gone to visit granny, back soon?'

'Except your granny is dead, Nelly, and the caves go on for a long time. There aren't any maps. Nobody knows where they go to or where they end.'

'You should have told me!'

'Perhaps. But I didn't know you very well, did I? And an old smuggler doesn't like to tell a stranger where he keeps his things. Besides, anything could have happened.'

'Exactly!'

'Perhaps you shouldn't have wandered off yourself?'

'That's none of your business!'

'First her husband, then her daughter. Poor thing.'

'But I came back!'

'Then floated off again in a hot-air balloon.'

'Because you lied to me!'

'Because I didn't want to upset you,' said the cabin boy, holding up his hands.

'You've upset me now alright!' shouted Nelly, jumping to her feet and drawing her cutlass. But just as she was about to express her feelings more directly, shots were fired outside the hut, the door flew open, and something hit her on the back of the head.

CHAPTER

TWENTY

When Nelly woke up, the fighting outside the hut was still going on, but she hardly noticed. She was too busy examining the sticks that made up the roof and the gaps between them. She did it in a dreamy way, because she was half awake and half asleep, which gave the things she actually concentrated on a special sort of clarity. The kettle on the stove. The teapot. The flowers on the tablecloth. Along the walls of the hut were shelves with various bits and pieces stacked along them, including a pair of climbing boots belonging to Nelly's grandmother: the empty boots that had been found on the mountain after the avalanche. Nelly did not have to think about it—if they were or if they weren't. She just knew, just as she knew that the tin sitting next to them was the cake tin Columbus had arrived in on her first birthday—a present from her father—a turtle still in his egg, cushioned by white sand from a faraway beach: the sand his mother had laid him in.

Nelly looked up and the yellow light filtered down, and everything was itself—the boots, the tin, the teapot. It was all a story that had started long ago, before she was born, and she was lying in the middle of it. The sticks were sticks. The gaps were gaps. The house was the downstairs house and outside a noisy fight was going on. She could hear people shouting and cursing, and the bang bang bang of their guns, which made her think of *The Bell-Hammer* and the Abuela's grey ships when she first met Ben. The boy on the buoy in the middle of the ocean, who had probably been eaten by a sea monster. Then she fell asleep for a little bit, and when she woke up the fighting was almost over. Only two figures continued to battle across the sandy floor, dancing around the rickety hut in which Nelly's parents had made their first home. The first was Aunt Barbara, unmistakable in her war wig and steel-capped boots.

'Traitor!' she shouted, 'Bandit!'

The second was the cabin boy, parrying with cutlass and pistol.

'Stop it, Barbara!' he was shouting, 'You're frightening me!'

'Butcher!' roared Aunt Barbara, 'Thief!'

'Will you please calm down and let me explain?'

'What is there to explain?' shouted Barbara, knocking the cutlass out of his hand. 'What is there to talk about? You're the Abuela! The smuggler-in-chief. You! My own nanny! And to think I let you sing me nursery rhymes!'

'Very well,' said the cabin boy, throwing down his pistol and falling to his knees. 'Kill an old man who loves you with his whole heart!'

'With pleasure!' said Barbara, and in the brilliant sunshine that now poured down the chimney, she raised her sword. But at that moment a voice boomed out, echoing off the walls of the bottle-shaped cave as if it were a stone trumpet.

'ENOUGH!'

And into the room, still wearing his diving suit, stamped the Admiral, with Ben trudging along behind him.

'Now will somebody please tell me,' he demanded, the tips of his moustache quivering with indignation and confusion, 'what on earth is going on?'

Next came lots of shouting. First Aunt Barbara, explaining why she wanted to kill the cabin boy (still kneeling in the sand), then the cabin boy, telling her how much he loved her, and asking her what, in any case, was the difference between a smuggler and a successful merchant? Did she even know what a smuggler was?

Then the Admiral.

'A smuggler?' he bellowed, 'I'll tell you what a smuggler is! A smuggler is a chap who doesn't care whose house he's in. Who comes in through the window instead of the door, or down the chimney. A chap with no family or honour, who creeps about in the dark, pocketing stolen property and selling it to anybody he pleases. A chap who doesn't pay his taxes, no better than a rat under the floorboards. That's what!'

'A rat?' shouted the cabin boy, looking up

from the sand. 'A rat?'

'Wait a minute,' said the Admiral, narrowing his eyes, 'don't I know you?'

'You should do! I joined your boat as a cabin boy. Worked in the kitchen. Looked after your children, and when their mother died, treated them as my own children. Comforted them, listened to their secrets, carried their messages. And then what? Dismissed! Out on my ear! Without a penny!'

'Quite right too! You're a scoundrel.'

'A scoundrel! A rat!' shouted the cabin boy, to the general assembly. 'See? Hear?'

And around the walls the smugglers added their own voices—'for shame!'—and even the crew of *The Bell-Hammer* began to mutter; a clamour that grew as the cabin boy listed his many services and the betrayal that had been his reward, asking the same question over and over again: 'A rat?'

Until the noise of the crowd became

deafening. A roar that drowned out the roar of the sea—the boom and hiss that gave the Devil's Ballroom its name. But Nelly didn't notice, because she had been watching a figure climbing down the stairs from the top of the chimney, threading the slender neck, then circling wider as it came closer. A tall, thin woman with something in her arms, walking slowly, making sure of each step because her feet were bare.

Down below the noise was approaching violence—revolution—but the woman was absolutely calm. She looked as though she had just stepped out of a bath, and was wearing a shower cap Nelly recognized.

'Mother,' she whispered.

And it was.

Penelope came down the stairs with a frown of concentration on her face, because she did not want to miss her footing, and the sunlight brightened her shower cap and the tops of her ears. It made her dressing gown shine with an almost blinding whiteness,

and at the same time it seemed to pass straight through her, casting no shadow, as if she were a ghost. But she wasn't. Nelly's mother walked in the pure midday sunlight, and one by one, as the people below saw her, they stopped shouting. They looked up with their mouths open—the Admiral, Ben, Barbara, the cabin boy, the smugglers with their long, grey hair, and the crew of *The Bell-Hammer* in green and gold. They stared in silence at the angel walking down the spiral stairs, holding something in her arms, and Penelope looked down at them with an absent smile, as if to say, 'oh, how nice, are you all here too?'

But she didn't actually say anything until she saw Nelly, looking out through the window of the hut, and then her face lit up properly.

'Oh darling!' she cried, coming towards her over the sand, 'there you are! We've been looking for you everywhere! And look, see? I've got Columbus!'

CHAPTER TWENTY-ONE

There was no room in the downstairs house for a proper family reunion, so they all went outside instead. Up the sides of the cave and out through the well in Nelly's back garden: the garden of the house she had lived in ever since she was a little girl, with the red roof and green windows. With the rhubarb patch and the apple tree and the rock pools full of crabs you could catch with a bit of bacon on a string.

But there wasn't enough room in the upstairs house, either, so they laid a banquet on the beach, and as arrangements were made to bring up tables and tablecloths, and everything else that was necessary for a really serious celebration from the

Abuela's well-stocked larder, everybody got re-acquainted. The Admiral (who had wept over his wife's empty boots) got down on his knees to beg his daughter's forgiveness, and was forgiven. Next came the cabin boy, although in his case the question of who should forgive who was more complicated. Aunt Barbara was still angry about the smuggling, and Nelly had not entirely forgotten the lie, but in the end it was decided that he should be appointed commander-in-chief of the Fiennes, Hillary, and Scott catalogue, with Ben as his right-hand-man, which meant that he could continue doing business exactly as before,

only with different stationery and a bit more paperwork.

'So I get to be a smuggler after all,' said Ben, happily, and as Barbara and her nanny embraced, he described the way the Admiral had saved him when the sea monster attacked the submarine.

'It tried to bite his head off, but he was wearing one of the Porbeagle family helmets. Then he stabbed it with his cutlass and it let us go.'

'Good for Grandpa!'

'Yes, he's all right. But I wonder how he'll manage without *The Kraken*.'

'He can live here with us. He can stay in

the lighthouse.'

And soon this also was agreed.

After supper Aunt Barbara made a toast to the Abuela's fleet and wished him every success as an honest trader.

'But I'll be keeping an eye on you,' she said, tossing her empty glass into the air and, whipping a pistol from her belt, turning it

to powder with a single, well-aimed bullet.

'Oh good shot, darling!' shouted Penelope (who loathed speeches), 'Bravo!'

Then the cabin boy spoke, then the Admiral, then Nelly, who said how happy she was to see them all—how delighted that everybody was alive and well—and then asked them all to look up at the stars, which were particularly beautiful that night. Stars like distant bonfires, together and apart at the same time.

And finally, when everybody else had gone to bed (some upstairs, some down), she went out to the end of the jetty with Columbus and her mother and sat looking at the moon.

'Where did you go?' she asked, dabbling her bare feet in the water.

'Where did I go?' replied Penelope, gently. 'I was here all the time.'

'But you weren't.'

'I was,' said Penelope, 'I just went downstairs to have a think.'

And she told Nelly what it had been like to be alone when Nelly had gone looking for her father, and her relief when the retired cabin boy arrived and turned out to be her old nanny. About the caves beneath the house, which she had forgotten, because they belonged to a different world.

'When I lived up here with you,' she said, 'I never thought about them at all, but when you left and Nanny came, I remembered. Then I started thinking about my mother, and all the plans we had made together, and I wanted to feel closer to her. So I wandered off for a bit on my own.'

'Do you think she's really dead?'

'I don't know. They never found her body, and down there in the dark, sometimes I thought she was talking to me. We'd even have little chats.'

'What about?'

'About you, and your father, and what you were doing. She told me not to worry. She said you'd be all right, because you were both brave and clever, and that I would be all right too. She said you loved me.'

She paused and stroked her daughter's hair.

'Do you know, when you first sailed away to find Captain Peabody, I thought I'd lost both of you. And then I asked myself: what would Nelly do in my position? So I knitted a balloon and drew a map and got ready to come after you. I even knitted you a flying suit.'

'I found it!' said Nelly.

'And just imagine how different everything would be if you hadn't. You would never have met the Admiral, or Ben or Barbara. We wouldn't be sitting here like this, with everybody back together again, even though you might have found me sooner. Isn't that strange?'

'Yes, I suppose it is, although I wish Papa

were here, too.'

'So do I,' said Penelope, and for a while they sat in silence, hand in hand, and Nelly thought how everybody had had their own adventure, and how nice it was that so many of them had come together at the same time and in the same place—Porbeagles and Peabodys and everybody else, all living beneath the stars, separate and together.

And then she thought of Captain Peabody, building his new ship across the water, and *The Kraken* lying in pieces at the bottom of the ocean, and the monster that had attacked them. If it was dead, or still lurking in the bay, or if it had gone back to the ooze at the bottom of the Challenger Deep. She thought of her balloon, floating on its own with nobody in it—which made her feel lonely, even though her mother was sitting right beside her and Columbus was snuggled in her lap.

But then Penelope squeezed her hand and pointed, and Nelly noticed that *The Bell-Hammer* had a visitor, concealed, though not quite hidden, by the night. A silky thread going up from the top of one of its masts to an unmistakable silhouette, long and sleek with tiny fins at its tail, printed against the moon. Carl— gentle, silent Carl—keeping Barbara and Ben company in the dark, and over to the right, beyond the moon's rim, a star burning a little brighter than the other stars: a flame which lit an answering flame in Nelly's heart, because it meant *The Sky Lantern* had also come home.

FIND OUT WHERE NELLY'S ADVENTURES BEGAN!

Nelly and the Quest for Captain Peabody

ONE GIRL.
ONE TURTLE.
ONE EPIC VOYAGE.

ROLAND CHAMBERS
ILLUSTRATED BY ELLA OKSTAD

ABOUT THE AUTHOR

Roland Chambers has had some adventures of his own. He's been a pig farmer, a film maker, a journalist, a pastry chef, a cartoonist, a teacher, a private detective, and an author. He's also lived in a few different countries, including Scotland, Australia, Poland, America, and Russia. Now he lives with a professor next to a cake shop in London. He owns two cats, three children, and two guinea pigs.

Ready for more great stories?
Try one of these ...

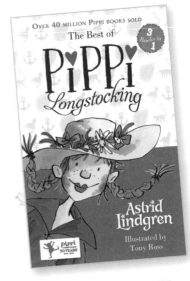